DORY

THIS BOOK BELONGS TO

_____

WARD

SHELDON

PEARL

Designed by Christine Jaszkowiak

Published by Scholastic Inc., 557 Broadway, New York, NY 10012,
by arrangement with Disney Licensed Publishing.
SCHOLASTIC, UNDERSEA SCHOOL, and associated logos are trademarks
and/or registered trademarks of Scholastic Inc.

ISBN 0-439-79886-8

12 11 10 9 8 7 6 5 4 3 2 1   5 6 7 8 9 10/0

Printed in the U.S.A.
First Scholastic printing, June 2005

FISH ARE FRIENDS, NOT FOOD

Adapted by Annie Auerbach

Illustrated by Disney Storybook Artists

SCHOLASTIC INC.

New York • Toronto • London • Auckland • Sydney
Mexico City • New Delhi • Hong Kong • Buenos Aires

Nemo and his friends were about to go on their first exploration to Kelp Canyon!

Marlin and Dory were their guides. First, Dory went over the safety rules.

"Rule number one: Never leave your buddy behind," she said. "Rule number two...uh...um..." Dory couldn't remember the rest of the rules!

Nemo and the other fish were listening closely—all except for Ward.

"I already know about safety. I could lead this group myself," grumbled Ward, who didn't see why they needed babysitters. "Let's get going!"

The group set off, but before long, they came across Bruce the shark.

"G'day!" he said.

"Aaaaaahhhhh!" screamed the young fish. They had never seen a shark up close before— especially one with such big teeth!

But Nemo quickly piped up. "Don't worry. Bruce is my friend. We're not in any danger."

"That's right, mate," said Bruce. "Fish are friends, not food."

9

Just then, a plant caught Marlin's eye. "Oh, kids!" he said. "I want to show you something very important."

"Now this plant is to be avoided at all costs," Marlin instructed. "If you touch it, it will cause an itchy rash. Ohhh. Ahhh!" Marlin got a funny look on his face. He began squirming around in the water, trying to scratch himself. He had accidentally touched the plant!

"I've got to get home,"
Marlin said, still scratching.
"Sorry, kids, we'll have to
cancel the trip. You can't go
without two leaders."

"Oh, no!" everyone cried.
"I can be a leader!" said Ward.
But the other fish just laughed at him.
Then Nemo had an idea. "What if
Bruce is Dory's co-leader?"

Marlin thought for a moment. "Well,
I suppose that would be all right. Just be
careful!" he yelled as he headed home.

Dory asked Bruce to join the class.

"I would love to help you, mates!" he said.

"I know a swell spot. It's better than Kelp Canyon.
How would you like to explore a sunken pirate ship?"

"Yeah!" exclaimed most of the fish.

"What about you, mate?" Bruce asked Ward. "Doesn't that sound exciting?"

"We don't need you. *I* know lots of good spots," Ward replied jealously. "And I'm *not* your mate!"

Before Bruce could answer, Nemo swam up between them and said, "Don't mind Ward. He's just a big know-it-all."

Of course, this made Ward really angry. "I'll show this shark who should be co-leader!"

Bruce led Dory and the young fish to the old sunken pirate ship.

"Here we are, mates!" Bruce said proudly. "Here's where I used to hang out when I was a mere nine-footer."

"Cool!" said Tad.

Nemo thought it looked a little scary and dangerous—but also very exciting. "I can't wait to go exploring!" he said.

15

Inside the shipwreck, the group got separated. When he realized that Bruce and Ward had both disappeared, Nemo sensed trouble.

Sure enough, he found them on the deck of the ship. Nemo wondered what Ward was up to. He watched closely.

"Bruce, I think I saw a fish stuck in that cage," Ward said.

"Really? Well, I've got to help him out—fish are friends, remember?" said Bruce, as he looked around inside the cage.

Ward quickly swam over to the latch on the cage and tried to close it, but it was stuck!

Nemo raced toward them. "Bruce! Look out! It's a trap!" he cried.

As soon as Bruce heard Nemo, he started moving and bumping around inside the cage. But instead of escaping, Bruce shook the latch loose. The cage door closed with a *SLAM!*

"Ward!" shouted Nemo. "You just locked up my friend!"

"Good!" Ward shouted back. "Now *I* can be the co-leader."

"Hey, mates, settle down," said Bruce.

"Don't tell me to settle down," Ward said. "You're locked up now, and there's nothing you can do about it." Ward sounded brave, but he was racing away from the cage as fast as he could. After all, Bruce did have very large teeth!

"Don't worry, Bruce. I'll help you out," said Nemo, trying to unlock the cage. But it was no use. The door was stuck.

"I'll get Dory. Maybe she can help. I'll be right back!" Nemo quickly swam off.

After searching through the ship, Nemo
finally found Dory and the rest of the fish.
"I need some help," Nemo said urgently.
"Ward locked Bruce up in a big cage."
"That's right," said Ward, who just swam in.
"We don't need him anyway! I can be the leader."
"You locked up Bruce?" Sheldon said
to Ward. "He's our buddy!"
"Yeah!" said the other fish.
"Bruce is our friend!"

"Uh…I was just trying to…" began Ward. He suddenly felt nervous and began backing away from the other fish. He darted beneath a floorboard to hide.

Then he got stuck!

All the fish tried to lift the board to pull Ward out, but they weren't strong enough. The board wouldn't budge.

"It's no use," said Ward with a grumble. "Just go home. I don't need anyone's help anyway."

"No way," said Nemo. "Rule number one is 'Never leave your buddy behind.' And *some* of us know how to follow the rules!"

"I'll bet Bruce could get him out of there," said Dory.

"But Bruce is stuck in a cage." Nemo reminded her.

"Oh, that's right," said Dory. "So, we'll just have to get him out first!"

Dory instructed the other fish to stay there—and stay together—while she and Nemo raced off.

At the cage, Dory and Nemo pushed and
pulled as hard as they could to get Bruce free.
But the cage door wouldn't open.

"Bruce, you've got to break free," said Nemo.

"Ford got himself stuck!" said Dory.

"That's *Ward*," Nemo corrected her.

"Yes! Ward!" said Dory.

"I know Ward's been really mean to you," Nemo said to Bruce. "But right now, he needs your help."

That was all Bruce needed to hear!
CRRRAAACKKK!!!
Bruce broke right through the cage!

Then, he swam over to Ward, and with his mighty strength—he freed him!

"Hooray!" shouted the other fish.

25

On the way home, Ward apologized to Bruce. "I'm sorry," he said. "I guess I have a lot to learn. I thought I was ready to be a co-leader."

"No worries," Bruce said kindly. "I shouldn't have taken you to such a dangerous place. It looks like we both have a lot to learn. So, are we mates?"

Ward was thrilled and relieved that Bruce wasn't mad at him. "Mates!" he said excitedly. After all, he never had a shark for a friend before!

A little later, Nemo swam over to Bruce. "Thanks for saving Ward, even though he was mean to you," he said.

"Aw, it was nothing, mate," replied Bruce. "Besides, that's what friends are for!"

The End